Jakob and the Ice Giant

CW00417889

Written by Sasha Morton

Illustrated by Edu Coll

It was an icy December day.

It's colder than usual.

That looks like a gem of some kind.

Jakob put the gem into his pocket and headed home.

Jakob didn't notice the white bird perched on the fence beside him.

In the dead of night, a thick frost fell over the city ...

... and a golden glow came from the gemstone by Jakob's bed.

Not much longer to wait, then the city will be mine!

The next morning ...

Days went by. The city fell silent as huge snowflakes landed on the frozen streets.

Everyone slept for longer and longer. The days were cold and gloomy.

The central heating still won't work. I'm getting ready for bed.

Just then, Jakob saw a pale bird land outside his window.

The graceful bird opened its beak.

Is that bird trying to speak to me?

Hey, bird! I'm deaf!

Yes, but I can read your thoughts!

Oh! I can hear you in my mind!

From the roof, Jakob could see that not even a mouse was awake.

Can you see those gigantic footprints?

Yes.

An ice giant is coming to destroy the city, but you can stop him with the gemstone!

The bird spread out her wings and grew so that Jakob could fit on her back.

In a flap of feathers, they were flying!

Moments later, they were skimming over the surface of an icy river.

I'll set you down gently

Jakob's eyes were stinging from the cold. Then he felt the ground shake.

Thud! Thud!

A heavy foot stamped on the boathouse!

What do I do?

Smash! Crash!

ROAR!

Hold up the gem!

Jakob's hand shook as he lifted the gemstone.

A ball of light made a bright, golden shield around Jakob and the bird.

The giant threw a tall pine tree into the river.

Jakob stood with a firm stance. The giant lifted up its foot and …

... spun around. He crashed into the woods and was gone.

Once they were in the air ...

They saw the giant just ahead of them.

They flew as close to the giant as they could.
Jakob took aim ...

The gem bounced off the giant's head.

The giant shattered into tiny shards of ice.

Jakob caught the gemstone before it hit the ground.

The city is safe!

The bird flew up through the ice. A rainbow glittered as the snow melted from the city streets.

The city was awake.

I never imagined this could happen to me!

Just as Jakob got back into bed ...

Jakob, the ice has gone ... and we still need bread for breakfast!

Phonics Practice

Say the sound and read the words.

/s/	c (e, i, y)

accent   December   city   icy   cyclone

/j/	g (e, i, y)

genius   gemstone   giant   giraffe   energy

/s/	-se

house   mouse   horse   nurse   purse

/s/	-ce

prince   palace   dance   stance   trance

Can you say your own sentences using some of the words on these pages?

What other words do you know that are spelled in these ways?

/e/	-ea

deaf   ready   feather   dread   instead

Common exception words

Mr   Mrs   through   eye   could   water

We may say some words differently because of our accent.

Talk about the story

Answer the questions:

1 What month was the story set in?

2 How were Jakob and the bird able to speak to each other?

3 What made the giant run away from Jakob?

4 Why did Jakob describe being deaf as his superpower?

5 How can you tell this is a fantasy story? What other fantasy stories do you know?

6 What would you like your superpower to be, and why?

Can you retell the story in your own words?